Tales from the Arabian Nights

Tales from the Arabian Nights

Retold by Lisa Commager
Illustrated by David Geva

NEW YORK

First published in this form in Great Britain by Orbis
Publishing Limited, London 1984

First published in USA 1984
by Exeter Books
Distributed by Bookthrift
Exeter is a trademark of Simon & Schuster, Inc.
Bookthrift is a registered trademark of Simon & Schuster, Inc.
New York, New York

ISBN 0-671-06805-9

Printed by Resopal in Portugal

Contents

Prince Ahmed

Once upon a time there was a king who had three sons named Hussein, Ali and Ahmed. He also had a beautiful niece named Nur. She lived in the palace with the king and princes, because her mother and father had died when she was a child.

When she was old enough to marry, the king decided to find her a husband, a prince from one of the neighbouring kingdoms. But he was surprised and alarmed to discover that all three of his own sons were madly in love with her.

'How can I let one of them marry her without making the other two unhappy and jealous?' he wondered. 'And what kind of kingdom would this be after my death if my sons are always arguing?'

Then he had an idea, and called his sons together.

'Boys,' he said, 'I realize that you are all in love with Nur.' They all nodded sadly. 'And you can't all marry her!' They shook their heads glumly. 'So I have decided to send you all on a long journey. You must stay away for a year, and at the end of the year you must each bring back the most wonderful gift you can find for the princess. It doesn't have to be the most expensive thing in the world – though I will give each of you plenty of money. It doesn't have to be the most beautiful thing in the world – though I have nothing against beauty. It doesn't have to be big, or heavy, or small or light – but it has to be special. Do as well as you can, my sons, and may the best man win.'

The boys were very pleased with their father's idea, which they found both generous and fair. So they packed some food and wine and a few clothes, and gratefully accepted the purses filled with gold which their father gave them along with his blessing. Then they took their horses, and rode off together. After five days they came to an inn. Hussein, the oldest, said, 'Let us go our separate ways now, but let us meet here in a year less five days. Then we will get home in exactly a year from the day we left.' So they embraced one another and went off in different directions in search of the perfect gift.

Prince Hussein went to a town on the sea-coast, for he thought that all kinds of exotic things would be arriving there in ships from far-off countries. He was not mistaken. Every shop was filled with different kinds of cloth, unusual earrings, necklaces, bracelets, exquisite statues in ivory and marble, and lovely rugs. Strange animals roamed the streets, acting as though they owned the town. Some of them played musical instruments while others listened. Some performed tricks, and some just sat in the sun like old men. Hussein felt quite blind and dizzy and decided to return to his inn. Just as he was turning about, a man walked past him carrying only one carpet and shouting, 'Who wants to buy this rug for only thirty thousand dinars?'

'Thirty thousand dinars!' exclaimed Hussein. 'That's a lot of money! What do you mean, *only* thirty thousand dinars?'

The man stopped and showed him the rug without saying anything.

'It's not very large,' said Hussein, 'and while it's true that it's nice, it's not *that* nice. How can you ask so much?'

'It's a bargain at the price,' replied the man. 'Do you know what this carpet can do? If you stand on it and tell it where you want to go, it will take you there instantly. You don't even need to say a magic word!'

'And will it take my horse too?' joked Hussein.

'And your horse. You can take a whole heap of horses if you want to.'

'May I try it out?' asked Hussein.

'Why not,' said the man. So Hussein stepped onto the carpet and wished himself at his inn. Suddenly there he was, in his room at the inn. 'Lucky I *didn't* have my horse with me!' he thought. He wished himself back at the market, and when he got there he paid the pedlar thirty thousand dinars, for he was sure that this carpet must be the most unusual and marvellous gift he could ever find for Nur. He still had almost a year to waste, so he settled down at the inn and enjoyed himself.

The second brother, Ali, made his way to a town called Shiraz, for an old merchant had once told him that Shiraz had the most marvellous market-place. Ali was not disappointed. On every side he saw richly embroidered tapestries, fine silks and precious gems.

'These things are beautiful,' he thought, 'but are they truly wonderful? What did my father mean by wonderful?' He was sitting in a cloth shop, brooding about the meaning of the word 'wonderful', when a pedlar walked in carrying an ivory tube in one hand and a crystal ball in the other. 'Tube and ball, only thirty thousand dinars,' shouted the pedlar.

'Goodness, that's a lot of money!' said Ali, laughing. 'Come and sit down with me and tell me how you can dare charge so much for such ordinary looking objects? Is it that you want to make them seem more valuable than they really are? Do you think rich people will be more tempted by your wares if they are overpriced?'

'No, not at all,' replied the man. 'These things are really very special. If you'll give me a cup of coffee I'll tell you about them.'

The prince gladly ordered more coffee and then the pedlar whispered, 'If you look through the tube and say out loud what you wish to see, a picture of it will appear in the crystal ball.'

'May I try?' asked Ali.

'Of course,' said the pedlar.

So Ali looked through the tube and said firmly, 'I wish to see my father,' and sure enough, there was a picture of the king in the crystal ball, looking well, but a bit bored.

'Surely,' thought Ali, 'this is the most wonderful present I could possibly buy for Nur.' So he gladly paid the pedlar thirty thousand dinars and then went back to his inn. He had a pleasant enough time in Shiraz, looking at beautiful things and drinking coffee, until one year less a week had passed and it was time to leave.

The youngest prince, Ahmed, also travelled to a big city, though it was not such a glamorous one. His city was inland, and was a market centre for the farmers who lived in the district.

Ahmed felt discouraged. He aimlessly followed a chicken which was following an old lady, until he found himself in the town's centre. There it was noisy and hot, and full of the smells of ripe fruit and rotting meat.

'I will never find anything truly wonderful here,' he thought. 'This is a dreadful place! I'd be better off looking in our palace gardens! What a fool I was to choose this place! I should have planned my trip more carefully.' And he decided to travel on. But just as he was about to leave his attention was caught by an old pedlar.

'Apple for sale, apple for sale, only thirty thousand dinars!' cried the man. 'Hurry, hurry, I have only one at this amazing price!'

Ahmed, laughing, stopped him. 'It certainly *is* an amazing price for an apple!' he said. 'How do you think you'll ever manage to sell it?'

'It's a *magic* apple,' said the man. 'If anybody gets sick, one sniff of this beautiful apple will cure him instantly.'

'If that's true, it's quite an apple,' said Ahmed. 'But how am I to believe you?'

By this time, a little group of people had gathered around them. A man said, 'My wife is dying, will your apple cure her? I can't pay you even one thousand dinars, but I would give my life to save her.'

'If this apple will cure this man's wife, I will pay you the full thirty thousand dinars for it,' said Ahmed.

So the pedlar, the husband and the prince set off together to the poor man's house and found his wife in bed, looking as though she had only hours left to live.

She clasped her husband's hand and smiled.

'Smell this apple, my darling,' he said, holding it up to her nose. As soon as she had smelled it, colour came back to her cheeks. 'I can't believe it! I'm well!' she said.

Ahmed of course bought the apple and bided his time in that town, wandering around and curing people, until the year was nearly over. Then he went to the inn to join his brothers.

How happy they were to meet again! They were all very excited, for each was sure that he had found the best present in the world to take back to Nur. At first, none of them would say what they had found, but that was difficult, because they weren't used to keeping secrets from one another.

'Oh, let's just all show what we've got,' said Hussein. 'It won't do any harm.' And he spread his carpet on the ground. 'I paid thirty thousand dinars for this!' he said. 'It looks pretty ordinary, doesn't it? But it will fly anywhere we want to go!'

His brothers were impressed.

'Well, this is what I got,' said Ali. And he showed the others his ivory tube and crystal ball. 'They don't look like much, I know,' he said, 'but I paid thirty thousand dinars for them. If you look through the tube, you see whatever you want to see in the ball.' And he looked. 'Oh, no!' he exclaimed, 'Nur is sick! She looks like she's about to die!'

They all gazed in horror at the picture in the ball.

'I'd better show you my present quickly,' said Ahmed, and he produced his apple. 'It looks like a normal apple,' he said, 'but I paid thirty thousand dinars for it. Anyone who is ill will get well if they sniff it.'

'Well, let's jump on my carpet and get back to Nur at once,' said Ali, and that is what they did.

They were back in the palace almost the moment they stood on the carpet. They leapt off their horses and rushed up to Nur's chamber. The king was sitting beside her bed, holding her frail hand and weeping. Nur was lying so still that the princes feared she was already dead. Ahmed held the apple to her nose. She was hardly breathing. But then her eyelids fluttered and she opened her eyes and sighed. She sat up, and colour came back to her cheeks, as though an artist had quickly painted them. She smiled.

'How lovely to see you all again, Ahmed, Ali, Hussein! But why am I in bed, when sunlight is pouring in through the window? And why are you all standing around me? And why is uncle weeping?'

The king embraced her, and everybody laughed for joy. Then the princes told the king and their cousin what had happened, and showed their presents.

The king looked pleased, but also troubled. 'Which of you has brought the most wonderful gift for Nur? The apple cured her, Ahmed. But without Ali's crystal ball

you'd not have known Nur was sick. Your crystal ball showed that she was sick, Ali, but without Hussein's carpet you could not have got here in time to save her; your carpet brought you quickly, Hussein, but without Ahmed's apple you could have done nothing for her when you got here. And so on. I will have to think of another way to find out which of you deserves her most.' He thought for a while. 'We'll have a shooting match!' he said. 'Whoever can shoot his arrow the farthest shall have Nur's hand in marriage.'

So the next day, at the stroke of dawn, the princes met out on the plain. The king sat nearby with Nur.

'I don't even know which one I want to win,' said Nur. 'I am so fond of all of them. They are all so good and kind and handsome, and they have all been my best friends for as long as I can remember.'

'Well, that's just as well,' said the king. 'It would be too bad if you set your heart on one of them and he lost. And I agree with you: any one of them would make you a fine husband.'

First Hussein drew his bow and released it. His arrow flew in a high arc and landed in a tree far away.

Next it was Ali's turn. His arrow landed in the ground just a few feet past the tree.

Then came Ahmed. His arrow went so far that it completely disappeared. The king and his sons spent hours looking for it, but to no avail.

'Well, what's lost is lost,' said the king. 'What can't be seen can't be counted. If we can't find it, we can't know where it went.' The king loved being logical. 'So Ali shall marry Nur,' he decided.

Hussein and Ahmed were both sad, but they considered their father's decision fair. Each of them embraced Ali and wished him and Nur a long and happy marriage. Then Hussein decided to travel around the world on his carpet, and to settle in some remote place where he could forget

Nur. Ahmed decided to search for his arrow, for he could think of nothing better to do.

Ahmed began from the place where he had stood to shoot the arrow. He walked in what he hoped was a straight line, looking to the left and to the right. He walked for miles.

'I could not possibly have shot my arrow this far,' he thought, as morning became afternoon. 'No man could! I must have missed it. Maybe I should retrace my steps.'

But for some reason he did not turn around, he just kept on walking. After many hours he was exhausted, for he had brought along nothing to eat or drink. He lay down on the hot sand to rest. He fell into a deep sleep, and when he awoke it was morning. He found he was lying next to a rock which had not been there before. And in that rock was stuck an arrow which he recognized as his own. He rubbed his eyes.

'How can this be?' he murmured. 'How can there be a rock and an arrow where there was nothing before? And how can an arrow be stuck in a hard rock? What is the meaning of it?'

Then he noticed near the rock a large brass ring which seemed to be planted in the ground. 'This is very strange!' he said. 'That ring certainly looks as though it wants to be pulled. But what could there be under the ground, except more ground? Maybe I should take my arrow home, if I can get it out of the rock. But it's too late now for me to marry Nur. Still, I think I should go home.' But even as he thought this, he was bending over the ring and pulling with all his might.

The ring came up, bringing with it a door which had been buried in the sand, and beneath the door there were steps leading down into the earth. As though in a dream, Ahmed went down the steps. At first it was dark underground, but Ahmed was not afraid. Then it became light, and he saw that he was in a kind of underground palace, full of treasures lying about as though nobody cared for them. He wandered for a while and came upon a beautiful woman, sitting very straight and still on a chair, as though she was waiting for something. When she saw Ahmed, she said, 'Ah, you've come at last, Ahmed! How glad I am to see you! I was afraid you might be lost.'

'Who are you, and how do you know my name?' he asked.

'I am called a peri, for I am the daughter of a powerful genie. I arranged your meeting with the pedlar who sold you the apple. I also chose your brothers' presents. But you were my favourite, so I made your arrow fly all the way here. I hoped you would find me. I was wishing that if you did find me you would want to marry me.'

'Oh, I do!' said Ahmed, for she had the sweetest face of any woman he had ever seen, and her voice was like music. He forgot Nur.

'I have been waiting for you for years,' she whispered. They were soon married, and for six months they lived together in perfect happiness.

But one day, the peri came home to find her husband looking sad. 'What's the matter?' she asked. 'Are you bored? Do I no longer please you?'

'You are my life,' said the prince, 'and you please me completely, but I can't help worrying about my father. I know he must be worried about me, because I set off only to find my arrow, and I never came back!'

Ahmed was right. His father was terribly unhappy. He had even asked a wise woman to find out where his son was. She had gone away for some days and said many magic spells, but when she returned to the king's court she could only tell him that Ahmed was alive and well – she could not find out where. 'He doesn't seem to be actually on this earth,' she said, 'though it is certain that he is not dead.'

The king was pleased, but he still missed his son. And Ahmed missed him. So the peri said, 'Ahmed, there is no reason why you shouldn't visit your father. But you must remember one thing. You must not tell him or anybody else where or with whom you are living, or our life together will end. Tell him only that you are happy and well. It is enough.'

Ahmed readily agreed, and set off with a light heart. His father was so glad to see him! 'Tell me all about what has happened to you in the last six months,' he said.

'I cannot,' said Ahmed, 'but I am happy and well, and I will come again.'

The king was satisfied and asked no more questions, and soon Ahmed returned to his wife.

All had gone well. The peri realized that Ahmed would never betray her, and she encouraged him to visit his father every month, which he did.

But the king's ministers began to be jealous of Ahmed, because he looked so happy. So they tried to find fault with him. 'He must live close by,' they said to the king, 'for his horses are always fresh. That shows he doesn't care for you; he would visit you every day if he did. He must be rich, because he brings you such splendid presents. We conclude, therefore, that he plans to seize your kingdom!'

That conclusion wasn't very logical, and the king loved logic, but still, after his ministers had gone on nagging him for a long time, his mind began to be poisoned with doubt and fear. He sent again for the old wise woman, and asked her please to try harder to find out where his son was.

She consulted her magic books for three whole weeks and found out where his arrow had landed. Then she went to that spot and lay down as though she were ill, and waited. After a few days, the prince came out of the underground palace, on his way to see his father. He found the old woman lying there and took her down to the peri, for he knew his wife could make anyone well.

The peri nursed the old woman for many days, and then the woman returned to the king and said, 'Your son lives in a magnificent underground palace, better than yours, with a beautiful and powerful peri. He might well overthrow your kingdom, for he could get all the genies to help him. Why don't you tell him you know he is married to the peri, and ask him to do some great thing for you, with the help of her powers. Then, if he succeeds, at least you've got some wonderful thing for yourself. If he fails, he'll be so ashamed he'll go away and stop bothering you.'

The king agreed, for he saw that either way no harm would come to anyone.

So the next time Ahmed visited him, the king said, 'I know that you have married a peri. Now if you love me I want you to prove her power and your love by having her make for me a tent which can be carried by one man, but which, when opened out, will cover a whole army. You know that every time I take my men into battle I have to provide camels, mules and horses just to carry the tents we need. It is too expensive.'

'I don't know how you found out that I am married to a peri, and I don't know how she can possibly fulfill your demand, but I will ask her,' Ahmed replied. And he returned to his own home.

'My heart,' cried his wife, 'why do you look so sad?'

'My father has found out about you,' said Ahmed. 'I don't know how –'

'That old lady told him,' said the peri.

'Maybe. Anyway, he wants you to create for him a tent which can be carried by one man but which will, when set up, cover a whole army. I don't know why he is asking the impossible of you.'

'People are afraid of what they don't understand,' said the peri. 'But don't worry, I'll make your father's tent. Come outside.' In a few minutes she was holding what looked like a large, red umbrella. When she shook it, it spread wide enough to cover three armies. 'It will be exactly the right size for any army,' she said, laughing at his astonishment. 'It can stretch for feet or miles, depending on what is needed.'

Ahmed took the tent to his father and displayed it, and not only the king but everyone at his court was struck dumb with amazement. But instead of being reassured, the king became even more anxious. 'If Ahmed's wife can make such a tent, how easy it would be for her to overthrow me!' he thought. So he called together his counsellors again, and they gave him some more terrible advice.

'I want you to prove your love for me by doing something even harder,' he said to his son the next time they met. 'Please bring me water from the Spring of the Crocodiles.'

Ahmed sadly returned to his peri. 'Everyone knows that it is most dangerous to attempt to get water from the Spring of the Crocodiles,' he said. 'My father asks too much of me. Please don't feel that you have to help me this time. It might be dangerous for you.'

'It will be easy for me, and for you, too,' said his wife. 'Take this bottle and three large hunks of meat. Tomorrow morning, get up early, and go out. You will see a fox roaming around. Follow the fox until you come to the three fierce lions who guard the spring. Throw the hunks of meat to the lions, and go past them as they are devouring them. After that, you will come to the lake. Stand on the snout of the biggest crocodile, and he will take you to the spring. Then you must fill the bottle with water from the spring. But be careful not to let a drop of water touch you, for if it does you will fall asleep for many years.'

Ahmed followed her instructions exactly, and returned safely with the water.

The king was impressed when Ahmed arrived with the water. But by this time his head had been completely turned by the advice of his wicked counsellors, and he no longer knew good from bad or right from wrong. In suspecting his own son of wickedness, and in trying to prove his suspicions well founded, the king himself had become wicked. By now, all he wanted was to see his son fail. So he asked something he was sure would be impossible.

'Bring me a little man with a long beard and a huge club, who is strong enough to destroy my whole kingdom. If you can do that, then I will believe you love me.'

'But father,' said Ahmed, 'why should I bring something so terrible into your world, even if I could?'

This only made the king angrier, for he now hated logic as much as he had once loved it. His mind seemed to have turned inside out and upside down. 'If you don't do as I say, I'll have you and your peri wife killed,' he said.

So Ahmed went sadly back to his wife and told her of the king's request. This time, she too was sad. 'I can do it,' she said, 'but I wish he hadn't asked it. It is my brother he wants you to bring. Don't be scared when you see my brother. He is horrible to look at, and he can be violent, but he will do no harm to those who wish him well.'

She lit a fire and mumbled some magic words, and out of the fire rose a monstrous man with a huge club. 'What do you want, sister?' he screamed in a bloodcurdling voice.

'Please follow my husband to his father's palace. And see that no harm comes to my husband.' The creature nodded, and he and the prince set out together.

As Prince Ahmed and the monster walked through the town, everyone who saw them fled, for the little man was the most horrible creature anyone had ever seen. The court had almost emptied itself by the time the two entered the palace. Fortunately, Ahmed's brother, Ali, and his wife, Nur, were upstairs and they saw nothing.

The king was poring over a book of black magic. When he looked up and saw the little man with the hideous face and the big club he began to tremble. 'I have brought upon myself my own destruction,' he said. 'Forgive me, son. I am no longer fit to rule, and I must depart, unless your friend chooses to kill me.'

The peri's brother just stood there and said nothing. Ahmed wept as he watched his father flee.

Then the little man disappeared into thin air. Ahmed went home to his beloved peri, and lived happily with her until they died. Ali and Nur became king and queen and they ruled the kingdom wisely and well.

Ali Baba and the Forty Thieves

Once upon a time, there lived in the city of Baghdad two brothers, one named Kassim and the other named Ali Baba. Their father, when he died, had left them an equal amount of money and land, which wasn't much, but Kassim had married a rich woman, and Ali Baba had married a poor one. Kassim and his wife were selfish and fat. They had no children, and they spent much of their time quarrelling. Ali Baba and his wife had one son, named Akbar, and although they were poor, they were a happy family. Kassim ran an oil shop, and became richer every day. Ali Baba was a woodcutter, and he earned barely enough to make ends meet. Nevertheless, when a poor girl named Morgiana lost both her parents and needed a home, it was Ali Baba and his wife who took her in and cared for her as if she were their own daughter.

But if Ali Baba ever asked his brother to lend him a little money, or even food, to help him get through the winter, Kassim only laughed and said, 'You should have thought about what it is like to be hungry before you married a poor woman; you should have thought about what it is like to be poor before you brought a son into the world;

and you should have thought about what it is like to be wretched and cold before you took an extra person into your family. You got yourself into this mess, now you can get yourself out of it.'

But, although Ali Baba's family was poor, it was never wretched. And when he told his wife he was sorry he could not do better by her, she smiled and said, 'Better to be poor and happy than rich and miserable.'

Every day, Ali Baba went high up into the hills to chop down trees or collect faggots to sell for firewood. The wood became scarcer as the years went by, but Ali Baba never complained – he just walked further to find it. It was a hard life, but Ali Baba loved being by himself in the woods every day, seeing birds and animals and different kinds of plants. He loved sitting with his back against a tree

and eating a chunk of bread and drinking some water from a nearby stream when it was lunch-time. And it was always nice to come home to his family at night.

Life went on in much the same way from year to year, with only the seasons and the children changing. Akbar grew up to be a bright and handsome lad, and Morgiana as she grew older helped more and more around the house. Ali Baba hardly noticed the passage of time, until one day something happened which was different from usual.

As he was cutting wood near some big rocks, Ali Baba saw in the distance a great cloud of dust. His donkey pricked up its ears, and Ali Baba stopped his work to listen. He heard distant hoofbeats getting louder and louder, and he realized that what he saw was not just a cloud of dust, but a long line of men approaching.

'These men can be up to no good,' he thought. 'So many men travelling together, they must be those thieves I have heard stories about, who wander about the countryside looting and pillaging and killing the poor people who get in their way.' Ali Baba quickly hid his donkey in a grove of trees and climbed a tree himself. He was just in time. They came riding up, yelling to one another, brandishing their swords, swearing and laughing loudly, acting as though they owned the world and would destroy it. Ali Baba was as still as a mouse.

The leader looked even more terrifying than the others. He stepped up to the rock in the side of the mountain and shouted, 'Open, Sesame!' There was a tremendous crash and the mountain opened, revealing a huge cavern. None of the men looked in the least surprised. Ali Baba, perched in his tree overhanging the rock, trembled and clung to the branch, hoping that the tree would not shake enough to be noticeable.

Then the men took their heavy sacks and entered the cave. The rock closed behind them. They stayed inside for some time, and then Ali Baba heard faintly from within the cry, 'Open, Sesame!' The rock drew open, and out came the men with their sacks empty. The rock closed and the men jumped on their horses, and galloped away.

Ali Baba sat dazed in his tree for a while after they had left. Could it all have been a dream? Surely not, for there were hoofprints smudged into the dust. There was one way to find out for sure, and that was to get down from his tree and pretend to be one of the robbers. 'Though of course,' he thought, 'if it doesn't work for me it won't prove it never happened. Maybe only the leader of the thieves has power over the rock. Still, it's worth a try.' So he did climb down, and he got his saddlebags, which he usually filled with light pieces of wood, from his faithful donkey who was still grazing quietly in his grove.

In a trembling voice, Ali Baba said, 'Open, Sesame!' and

although he had hoped it would, he was as astonished as though it were the first time he had seen it happen when the rock swung open with a thunderous crash. 'Even for me!' he murmured, and smiled to himself. He looked around. There was no one in sight except his donkey. 'Stay here, my pet,' he said, 'I'm going in.'

He crept down some steep steps, deep, deep under the ground. He heard the door crash shut behind him. The cave was dark, but the thieves had left one lamp burning, and the light from it was caught up in brightness everywhere by heaps of glittering gold. Ali Baba rubbed his eyes. 'Surely this *is* a dream,' he said. As his eyes grew accustomed to the dark, he saw that the walls of the cavern were hung with exquisite carpets. Strewn about on the floor were pearls, diamonds and other precious stones. Ali Baba picked up a gold coin. It did not disappear at his touch, nor did it burn his hand. Then he started dumping gold and jewels and other treasures into his saddlebags as fast as he could. 'For surely it is no sin to steal from thieves!' he told himself. When his bags were full, he lugged them up the stone steps and cried, 'Open, Sesame!' The rock sprang open and he staggered out with all his riches. His faithful donkey was waiting for him at the entrance to the cave. Ali Baba waited until nightfall. Then he loaded the donkey, and together they walked down the hill back to the sleeping town.

Ali Baba's wife wasn't sleeping though. She was frantic with worry. 'Where have you been?' she cried.

'Shhh,' whispered Ali Baba. 'You will know soon enough.' And while she made him some supper, he told her all about his adventure. 'But you must promise never to tell a soul,' he warned her. 'For if the thieves find out that I am there, they will kill us with their sharp swords. I am going to bury the treasures in a hole. When we need them, we will be able to get at them, but the ground will keep them secret for us until that time.' Then he dumped some of his plunder out onto the straw mat they slept on.

His wife's eyes looked as though they would pop out. 'We are rich, Ali Baba!' she whispered.

'Yes,' he said, 'we will never have to fear hunger again. But remember what I said. Never tell a soul.'

'Oh, I promise I won't!' his wife replied. 'But now let us count the coins.'

'There are too many to count, it would take too long. Let us just bury them quickly, and be thankful that we have too much to count.'

'Oh, please,' begged his wife, 'if you won't let me count the coins, can't I at least weigh them? I want to have some number I can keep in my head, so I will be able to tell myself exactly how rich we are.'

'Where are you going to get the scales?' asked Ali Baba.

'From Kassim's wife. I promise not to tell her anything!'

'All right, if you must,' said Ali Baba, for he wanted his wife to be happy. But his heart was full of foreboding.

So the next morning, Ali Baba's wife rushed off to the other woman to borrow her scales. 'What for?' asked Kassim's wife. 'What do you have that's worth weighing?'

Ali Baba's wife only pursed her lips tight shut. This made Kassim's wife even more curious, so she smeared some honey on the bottom of the scales before she gave them to her sister-in-law. 'Whatever she is weighing, a little bit will stick to the tray so I'll know,' she thought.

Ali Baba's wife thanked Kassim's wife and hurried home. She weighed the gold coins and found that they were just as heavy as she had hoped, and maybe even heavier. Then she let Ali Baba bury them in the ground.

As soon as the gold was buried, Ali Baba's wife rushed back to the other woman's house with the scales, for she wanted to show what a good sort of borrower she was. Kassam's wife had always looked down her nose at Ali Baba's wife and treated her as though everything she did were wrong.

'Here are your scales!' said Ali Baba's wife brightly, and stood around, expecting to be invited for a cup of coffee.

'Thank you,' said Kassim's wife. 'You may go now.'

As soon as Ali Baba's wife was gone, Kassim's wife examined the scales to see what kind of grain had been weighed. Imagine her surprise when she found, stuck to the bottom of the scales, not a grain of barley or rice, but an old gold coin!

'Kassim,' she bellowed, 'Come here!' He came. 'Your brother has been deceiving you all these years,' said the woman, 'trying to make you feel sorry for him because he's poor! Look at this! He's so rich he has to weigh coins to see how much he has! I'm glad we never gave him anything when he asked for help! What a crook he is!'

Kassim gazed at the coin. 'This is unbearable!' he said, and ran all the way to his brother's house.

'What is the meaning of this?' he shouted. 'How dare you pretend to me that you are a poor man when you are weighing the likes of this? You must have so much gold you can't even count it! You're a miser, that's what you are! You should have been helping *us* all these years!'

Ali Baba was appalled. The only way he could defend his honour was to tell his brother the truth. So he told him all about the forty thieves, and the mountain that opened when it was told to.

'I don't believe you,' said Kassim. 'Which rock in which mountain?'

So Ali Baba had to tell him that.

'And what were the words you used?'

'Open, Sesame,' said poor Ali Baba. 'But I will give you one half of my gold and a beautiful necklace for your wife and a silver bowl for your cat if you will promise not to tell anybody.'

'I have no intention of telling anybody, and you can keep your silly old stuff,' said Kassim. 'All that remains in the cave will be mine. You stay away from there from now on, you hear?'

'I planned to stay away,' Ali Baba replied quietly. As his brother left, Ali Baba looked after him sadly. 'My dear wife,' he said, 'you needed to know too much, and now we may lose everything.'

'I'm sorry, Ali Baba,' she wept, and he comforted her.

Kassim told his wife the whole story, though he kept the magic password to himself. 'So by tomorrow, we'll be even richer than Ali Baba!' he said triumphantly.

Before the sun rose the next morning, Kassim set out with three mules and plenty of empty sacks.

When he got to the rock, he looked around to make sure he was alone, and then said in a firm voice, 'Open, Sesame!' He couldn't help being surprised when, with a thunderous roar, the mountain split open.

In he rushed, and set to work collecting the first things he came upon, silver coins. But as he made his way further into the cavern, he saw that there were thousands of gold coins, so he dumped the silver ones and took gold ones instead. He wandered on, and came upon a heap of diamonds, rubies and pearls. So he dropped his gold coins and filled all the containers he could find with precious

jewels. By this time, he was overwhelmed by all the dazzling splendour, and dizzy with exhaustion. 'I've got enough for one day,' he decided, and staggered back to the entrance of the cave.

'Open, Barley!' he cried. Nothing happened.

'Open, Wheat!' Nothing.'

'Open, Peanuts!' Silence. Kassim began to get scared. He racked his brain for the right word, but the one word that wouldn't come into his mind was 'sesame'.

He stood there shivering in the dank, dark cold. All of his newly found treasures seemed pretty useless to him now. He kicked a marble statue across the ground but it didn't break, it only hurt his foot. Then he heard the clattering of what sounded like horses' hoofs, faint at first, but getting louder and louder. 'There must be a lot of horses, if I can hear them through this stone,' he thought. And then he remembered, 'forty'. He heard a muffled shout, 'Open, Sesame!'

'Sesame,' he thought, 'that's the word,' and in the same instant the thieves were upon him. They cut off his head and left it in the entrance to the cave. Then they carried their new plunder in, stepping over his body as they went in and out. But their leader was furious, and swore he'd find out how this stranger had found his way into their precious secret place.

Kassim's wife, meanwhile, was waiting impatiently for him to bring back the treasure. When the sun was high in the sky, she began to be anxious. By the time it was setting, she was frantic. And after it was dark, she ran to Ali Baba's house, beside herself with worry.

'Where is my husband?' she wailed.

'I don't know!' replied Ali Baba.

'He left before dawn this morning. He should have been home before lunchtime! I don't care about the stupid gold, but I must have my husband! Please get him for me – you are the only person who can!'

'You don't even have to ask,' said Ali Baba, 'after all, he is my brother.' And although it was late, he got on his donkey and rode off to the mountain. 'Open, Sesame!' he cried, when he got to the rock. The mountain burst open to reveal his brother in two pieces.

'Oh my poor, poor brother,' moaned Ali Baba. 'How could they have done this to you?' Forgetting how cruel

his brother had always been to him, and remembering only that they were brothers, Ali Baba decided that he must give Kassim a decent funeral. He knew it was crazy to take his brother's broken corpse away, because it would show the thieves that there was somebody who was still alive who knew the magic word. But he did it anyway. Soon he was at home with his terrible burden. Luckily, his brother's wife had returned to her own house. His wife and Akbar and Morgiana gathered around him, and he sadly showed them the remains of his brother.

'How are we to tell his wife?' Ali Baba's wife sobbed. 'It's all my fault for wanting to weigh that awful gold.'

'Leave everything to me,' said Morgiana. 'I have an idea that might work. First, I will go and tell Kassim's wife that Kassim is safe, but can't come home just yet.' And this she did. Next, she asked Ali Baba if he would give her twenty gold pieces, so she could carry out her plan. He readily gave them to her. Then she went to the other end of town and entered the dusty little shop of an old tailor whom she had known when she was a small child. He was a good tailor, but he was also something more – a magician. Morgiana was the only person in Baghdad who knew about his magical powers. She had once, as a child, overheard him fighting with the King of the Demons. The King of the Demons had been angry at the tailor for having magical powers, and had told him to stop practising magic. The tailor had stopped, out of fear, but he had been very poor ever since. Morgiana thought maybe she could persuade him to help Kassim and the rest of the family, if she offered him enough money.

Morgiana told the tailor that she had a cousin whose head had been cut off in a dreadful accident. 'Please,' she said, 'won't you sew it on again? I'll pay you well.'

'Yes,' said the tailor, 'I can do that.'

'And you'll bring him to life? I'll pay you well.'

'Oh, if I must,' sighed the magician. He was so poor he was hungry most of the time, and besides, he missed practising magic. Morgiana thanked him and tied a blindfold around his eyes, so he wouldn't know where she was taking him. She didn't remove the blindfold until they were safely in Ali Baba's house. The magician sewed Kassim's head back onto his body, and then said a spell. They all waited with bated breath – and suddenly Kassim opened his eyes and said, 'What am I doing here?'

'Hurray, it worked!' cried the magician, dancing with glee. Morgiana gave him the twenty gold coins, blindfolded him, and took him home again.

Well, you can probably imagine how pleased Kassim was to be alive again. Indeed, he seemed to be a quite different man. 'My dear, dear brother,' he said, 'I have always been so mean to you, and you have been so kind to me!'

'It is mainly Morgiana who is responsible,' said Ali Baba. 'And the tailor. I only brought you here. Morgiana found a tailor who is a magician friend of hers from when she was little, and he fixed you up.'

Kassim thanked Morgiana, and begged her to thank the tailor for him. 'But *you* came and got me,' he said to Ali Baba, 'and I tried to do you out of a fortune.'

'But I didn't want any more treasure! I have enough!' said Ali Baba.

'I don't want any at all now,' said Kassim, laughing and shivering. 'In fact, I want to take my wife and go far away from here, to a place where I will never possibly see the faces of those robbers again. You, my dear brother, if you can bear to stay here, must do me the honour of accepting my olive-oil store. And please forgive me for the way I've treated you.'

'There is nothing to forgive!' said Ali Baba, 'and I accept the store with pleasure.'

Kassim went home to his wife, who was delighted to see him but not surprised, since she didn't know he'd ever been dead.

'We are going to start a new life together,' he told her, 'and we are never going to quarrel again.' So they went off happily, waving goodbye to Ali Baba, his wife, his son and Morgiana. Then Ali Baba and Akbar took over the store and did a thriving business.

Ali Baba had no desire to go back to the cave. He was very happy being an olive-oil merchant. But when the thieves returned to the cave and saw that Kassim's body was gone, they realized that somebody beside themselves was still living who knew the magic password. And naturally they assumed that whoever it was would be coming back all the time for gold if they didn't stop him. So their leader wandered around the city asking people if there had been a funeral recently (it never occurred to him that Kassim might have been put back together again).

Everyone said there had been no funeral. The bandit was puzzled. Why would anyone go to all the trouble of rescuing a dead man if not to give him a proper funeral?

Just as he was about to give up hope, he came to the tailor's little shop, and for some reason found himself stopping in front of it. The tailor was singing as he worked. The leader of the thieves entered the shop. 'Why are you singing, my good man?' he asked.

'Why not?' replied the tailor. 'I'm happy! I'm a fine tailor, who's been paid well for a difficult piece of work!'

'And what was that?' asked the thief.

After being silent for so many years about his powers, the tailor suddenly had an urge to boast. 'I sewed a man's head to his body!' he said, and then he told the thief the whole story.

'If I paid you well, could you take me to that place?' asked the thief.

'No, for I was blindfolded.'

'But if I blindfolded you again, and gave you ten gold pieces as a reward, could you take me there?'

'Maybe I could,' replied the tailor.

The thief covered the old man's eyes, and they walked together until they reached Ali Baba's house. 'Here we are,' said the tailor proudly, and the thief thanked him and gave him ten gold coins. After the tailor had gone, the man took a piece of red chalk from his robe and put a big red cross on Ali Baba's house. 'Tomorrow,' he said to himself, 'I will send the others to kill everyone in this house. Then there will surely be no one left who knows the magic words except us!'

When Morgiana came home from market that afternoon she noticed the red cross, and knew at once what it meant. She waited until night fell, and then, under cover of darkness, she went up and down the street marking all the houses with red chalk. Naturally, when the men arrived, they had no way of figuring out which house was the right one, so they had to return without bloodshed.

'You fools,' shouted the robber chief, 'You idiots!' But of course he knew perfectly well that it was not his men's fault that they couldn't find the right house. 'Somebody knows too much,' mused their leader. 'Somebody is too clever.' And he realized that he himself had been stupid not to remember what the house looked like, instead of just putting a chalk-mark on it and sending his men to do the dirty work.

So he had to return to the tailor.

'Please, he said, 'would you mind taking me again to that house?'

The tailor laughed. 'Is this your way of getting exercise?' he asked.

The thief glared at him. He was furious that a mere tailor dared to insult him, but what could he say? 'Fifty gold pieces,' he said.

'Oh, for fifty gold pieces I'll gladly let myself be blindfolded and I'll gladly take you there,' said the tailor. 'And what are you planning to pay me to do it again tomorrow?'

The thief was speechless with shame and anger. He gave the tailor fifty gold pieces, and the tailor again led him to the house. This time, instead of marking it, the thief studied the house carefully from all angles.

Later, when he was back in the woods with his fellow thieves, he presented his latest plan. 'I am going to put the thirty-nine of you into large jars. Of course they will have special slits in the lids so you can breathe. Then I'm going to load you on to twenty camels. The fortieth jar I'm going to fill with oil, and I shall ride with that one. Now, when we get to the house of this man who knows our secret, I'll find a way to leave you in your jars in the courtyard. I'll also find a way to spend the night in this man's house. But you must all stay awake, and when I come out and tap on the jars you must all leap out at once and kill everybody in the house. Is that clear?'

'It certainly is,' said one of the thieves. 'We do all the work while you have the fun.'

'What?' shouted the chief of thieves.

'Nothing,' said the man.

All the other thieves thought it was a splendid idea to get into jars and pretend to be olive oil. 'It will be very restful,' one of them said. They all went to market to buy the jars, and that evening, thirty-nine of them hopped into the empty jars and waited. It was not long before their leader had hoisted them all onto the poor camels. Then he mounted the camel with the last jar, which really did contain olive oil, and he set off. All the other camels fell into line behind him with their heavy burdens.

When the thief, followed by his long procession, arrived late at night at Ali Baba's house, he knocked at the door and waited. Ali Baba answered. 'Oh, good sir,' said the thief, 'I have come a long, long way today with my forty camels, and they are tired, for they are carrying two jars of olive oil each.' He lifted the lid of the jar his camel was carrying, and showed Ali Baba the olive oil. 'I too am tired. Would it be possible for me to rest my camels in your courtyard, to free them from their burdens for a while?'

Ali Baba was delighted, because now that he had himself come into good fortune, he was always looking for ways to share his wealth and happiness with others. 'Please do put your camels in my courtyard, and let them stretch their poor backs and have some food and drink. And you, my good man, must come in and dine with me! You are most welcome!'

So, the thief unburdened his camels and gave them some food from Ali Baba's stables. Then he joined Ali Baba inside. Morgiana brought the two men plenty of wine to drink, and they told each other stories while she prepared an enormous and elegant meal.

But shortly after she started cutting up the vegetables, Morgiana noticed that they were almost out of cooking oil. 'I'm sure the merchant won't mind if I take just a little from one of his jars,' she thought. 'I don't want to interrupt the men to ask him about such a little thing.' So she took a ladle and went out to the courtyard.

As she lifted the lid of one of the jars, she heard a voice murmur, 'Is it time for us to come out and kill the people now? It's getting uncomfortable in here!'

Morgiana nearly froze with horror, but she pulled herself together quickly and whispered, 'Not yet!' Then she looked around at the other thirty-eight jars with wide, scared eyes. Suddenly she had an idea. She ran to Ali Baba's store and brought back a fresh barrel of oil, rolling it along the street. She used a pitcher to transfer the oil to a huge pot, and brought it to boil over the fire. Then she ladled the boiling oil into a jug, took the jug to the courtyard, and poured the oil over the thief, killing him instantly. This she did thirty-eight more times, until all the thieves in the jars were dead.

Now there was only one thief left to dispose of, but he was the worst and most dangerous, as Morgiana knew, for it was clear that the man who was safe inside her master's house, drinking her master's wine, was the organizer of the whole plot. Morgiana stood in the silent courtyard for a while, trying to figure out what to do. Then she knew. She went in and dressed in a lovely dancing costume. Ali Baba was astonished when he saw her dancing in without a meal! It wasn't like Morgiana at all. She danced beautifully, and for a long time, and she saw that the chief of thieves was getting very restless. Finally, she held out a sword with the flat side up, as women who danced for money did. Ali Baba was shocked, but he put a coin on the sword. Morgiana danced over to the thief, and as he reached for a coin, she plunged her sword through his heart.

'Morgiana!' shouted Ali Baba. 'Have you gone mad? How could you kill a guest in my house? You, who are reasonable, intelligent, sweet and kind – you have committed the worst of crimes!'

'Do not worry, my master,' said Morgiana. 'This man was the chief of the forty thieves whom I overheard you telling your wife about. He was planning to kill you, and your wife, and Akbar, and me. If you do not believe it, come and look at his jars of oil in the courtyard.' And

Morgiana showed him that there was oil in only one jar, and told Ali Baba what the first man had said when she opened the lid. 'I don't like the idea of killing anybody,' she ended up, 'but I think the world is better off without these men, who have already killed scores of people, and who were about to kill us.'

'You have saved our lives,' said Ali Baba. 'You must be the most intelligent young woman in the world, as well as the kindest, bravest and prettiest.'

'I agree,' said his son Akbar, who had been keeping out of the way all the time.

'And now I have an idea,' said Ali Baba. 'Why don't you marry Akbar?'

'That's a wonderful idea, and one which has passed through my mind many times,' said Akbar.

Morgiana smiled sweetly and said, 'Thank you.' It was an idea that had passed through her mind once or twice as well, but she didn't want to say so.

So they were soon married, and Ali Baba gave them his brother's olive-oil store as a wedding present. The whole family went on living happily as before.

Aladdin and the Magic Lamp

Long ago in China there lived a poor widow with her son, Aladdin. He was a useless boy who never did anything except loll about in bed, or play with his friends in the street. Whenever his mother asked him to help her with the housework, or to go to the shops for food, he would say, 'Tomorrow, mother,' or 'Maybe later, when I've finished what I'm doing.'

One day, a powerful magician from Morocco, in Africa, happened to be walking along the street when he saw Aladdin hanging around with a bunch of other boys, giggling and snickering and making faces at old ladies who passed by.

'My, my,' thought the sorcerer, 'that certainly looks like about the most worthless boy I've ever seen! He may be just the one I'm looking for!' And the man beckoned to one of Aladdin's friends and asked him who Aladdin's father was, and where he lived.

The boy told him that Aladdin's father was dead, and that he lived with his mother in a little hovel on the outskirts of town. The sorcerer was delighted.

That night, as Aladdin and his mother were about to sit down to a bowl of rice, there was a knock on the door. The poor woman opened it, and there stood the magician. 'My dear, dear lady,' he said, 'how wonderful, after all these years, how very happy I am to see you! And your lovely son! But where is my brother? I have come all this way to see Mustafa, my long-lost brother!'

'But Mustafa was my husband. I didn't think he had a brother. And he's dead!' The woman replied.

'Oh, no, then I am too late.' The magician began to weep great big tears.

'I didn't know he had a brother,' the woman repeated.

'Ah, well, now you know. I have always wanted to find Mustafa again so I could share my good fortune with him. Still, he left a son. Pray let me help the poor boy. What is your trade, boy?'

Aladdin hung his head. 'I have no trade.' he said. For the first time he felt ashamed of himself.

'We'll take care of that!' said the magician. 'Tomorrow I'll take you to town and buy you some fine clothes, and then I'll set you up in a shop. You and your mother will soon be rich!'

And the next day, the magician really did take Aladdin to a shop, and he bought him the most beautiful clothes. After that, they strolled through the streets together and then wandered in the gardens which lay at the edge of the city. Aladdin was very happy.

They walked on beyond the gardens until they reached a mountain. Aladdin was exhausted. 'Here we stop,' said the magician. 'You may rest awhile while I light a fire.' So Aladdin sat down and idly watched as the strange man laid the fire. But when the sorcerer threw incense into the fire, and uttered a magic spell, Aladdin leapt to his feet in shock; there was a clap of thunder and the mountain split open before his very eyes. A stone slab with a brass ring was suddenly revealed.

Aladdin started to run away, but the sorcerer grabbed him. 'Oh no you don't, you silly little boy! You stay right here and pull that ring. You'll find inside a cave full of marvellous treasures! You must go down into the cave, through three great halls and a garden full of false fruit trees, until you come to a harmless little monster with a worthless little lamp on its back. You are to pour the oil out of the lamp and bring it to me. You can pick some fruit from the trees on your way back if you like, but you mustn't touch anything else. Here, take this ring to wear on your finger, it will bring you luck.'

'But uncle, how can I possibly lift that heavy stone?' whimpered the boy.

'Only you *can* lift it, you fool,' snarled the sorcerer. 'Only you and nobody else. And if you do as I say, you will soon be rich. Go on! Don't be a scaredy cat!'

Aladdin's greed overcame his fear, and he pulled on the brass ring which was attached to the stone. To his great surprise, the stone slab moved easily, and beneath it were revealed steps leading deep into the earth. First he passed through a room brimming with treasures, then a hall filled with the most luminous of fruits, which he thought were made of glass. Finally, he came to the monster with the lamp on its back. He seized the lamp, poured out the oil, and stuffed it into his robe. Then, stopping often on the way to fill his pockets and hands with the lovely-looking fruits, he staggered back to the mouth of the cave.

'Quick, give me the lamp!' screamed the sorcerer.

'I will,' said Aladdin, 'but for goodness' sake, help me out of here first!'

'No, you give me that lamp first!'

But Aladdin couldn't even get at the lamp, which was tucked into his clothes, because his hands were full of the fruits he had collected. 'Please, uncle, let me out of here!' he begged, and managed to hold out one hand for a moment.

The magician was in a rage. He thought that Aladdin had discovered the value of the lamp and was planning to keep it for himself. In a terrible frenzy, the nasty little man threw some more incense into the fire and yelled a curse on the boy. The stone slab swung back over the cave, and Aladdin was trapped.

Now the magician and Aladdin were both miserable. The magician had spent twenty years working out a way to find this magic lamp and the lazy boy named Aladdin.

His magic books had informed him that Aladdin was the only person in the world who could open the cave and get the lamp. And at the last minute his plans had been foiled by the boy's stubbornness. What was even worse, the sorcerer had forgotten to get his ring back, and without it he was almost helpless as a magician. He walked away moaning, empty-handed, and made his way back to Africa.

The boy was in an even worse fix, or so it seemed. For two days he wept, and nearly starved, for the fruits he had collected were not for eating. Then something strange happened. Late on the night of the second day, he rubbed his hands together in grief, and twisted the ring on his finger. Suddenly a huge genie appeared.

'I am the genie of the ring. I help anyone to go where he wants to. Would you like to go anywhere?' he boomed, in a voice louder than thunder.

Aladdin, having lived close to death for two days, wasn't afraid at all. He said, 'Oh please, take me home to my mother!'

The cave opened, and Aladdin found himself standing beneath the mountain. The next thing he knew, he was at home. His mother embraced him, and asked him no questions. She gave him all the food she had, and then he emptied his pockets, and went to sleep.

When he woke up, Aladdin was dreadfully hungry again – after all, he had been for two whole days without food, and had a lot of catching up to do. But his mother sadly told him she had no food left in the larder.

'Then we'd better sell this old lamp,' said Aladdin. 'And after that, mother, I'll learn a trade and be a better son to you.'

'First we must polish it or nobody will even look at it,' said Aladdin's mother, and she set to work, rubbing the lamp with a cloth. What was her astonishment when, larger than life and five times scarier, a huge blue creature appeared. 'I am the genie of the lamp,' it roared. 'What can I do for you?'

Aladdin's mother fainted, but Aladdin was getting used to genies, so he replied, 'Please bring us the best meal you can imagine.' In no time, the genie had disappeared and returned with a meal fit for a king and queen. The food was served up in gold dishes, lots of them, and there were silver

goblets filled with wine. Aladdin's mother had recovered by this time, and she and her son sat eating and drinking and laughing and talking for many hours. Aladdin told her all about his journey with the man who had pretended to be his uncle.

'I hope he boils in oil!' said Aladdin. 'I hope he gets eaten by a purple genie!'

'Now, now,' said his mother, 'calm down. You are still alive and well, and we've had this marvellous meal, partly thanks to that man. But my son, I think we must get rid of the lamp. It is too good to be true, so it must be bad. It makes me feel guilty to enjoy myself so much. And besides, I don't like having a genie like that in the house, even if he is nice.'

'Oh, mother, it wouldn't make sense to get rid of the lamp. We just won't use it unless we have to. We'll sell these gold plates and silver goblets, and I'll try as well to find a way to earn some money.'

So when their food ran out, Aladdin took one plate to the market and sold it for a little money. Then he took a goblet, and sold it for enough money to buy another meal. But one day, an honest jeweller stopped him in the street and asked to see his wares. 'This is worth a lot of money!' he said to the boy, holding up a small plate. The jeweller gave him seventy dinars for the plate, and Aladdin and his mother were able to live in comfort for a long time.

Aladdin began to be interested in gold and silver and precious gems, and he often went to visit the jeweller to talk to him and examine his wares. One day as he was looking at sapphires and rubies he remembered the 'fruits' he had brought out of the cave, and realized with a shock that they were not glass trinkets at all, but precious gems. Still, he did not forget that he had promised to work for a living, and he never wanted to see his mother suffer poverty again, so he kept the fruits hidden, and became an apprentice to the jeweller, so that he could be an evaluator of jewels. Soon he was well known and much respected in the city's market-place.

One day, as he was talking to his friends, a herald ran through the streets shouting that all the people were to close their shops and their eyes while the princess went past on her way to the baths.

'I wonder if she is really as beautiful as people say she is?' mused Aladdin. 'Maybe they are making us hide our eyes because she is ugly, and they don't want us to know!' He was overcome by curiosity, so instead of going inside a shop he climbed to the roof of the bath-house, so he could watch her going in without himself being seen. When she passed through the door, he was astounded. Her skin was like ivory, her hair like blackest ebony, her lips curved like an angel's, and her eyes shone more brightly than the most precious jewels. Aladdin fell instantly and wildly in love with her. He returned home, and for days would neither eat nor drink, but lay on his bed, gazing at the ceiling.

Well, Aladdin went on that way until his mother couldn't stand it any longer. 'Listen, my lamb,' she said, 'you've got to eat! What can I do to make you eat? What can I do to make you happy?'

'There is only one thing in the world that can make me happy,' he replied. 'That is to marry the princess.'

'You must be joking!' said his mother. 'I know you are the handsomest, most intelligent boy in the world, but you must remember that your father was a poor tailor, and I am a poor and simple seamstress. And you – well, you haven't really done anything in you life except hang around the market looking at jewellery. Which is, of course, fine as far as it goes, but –'

'That is all very true,' said Aladdin, 'but if I can't marry her I shall die.'

'But you have no wealth to offer her, and no title!'

'Ah, you'd be surprised,' said Aladdin. 'I haven't been judging the value of jewellery for nothing. Take a look at these again, mother.' And from under his bed Aladdin brought the jewels he had collected in the cave. They filled the room with many colours of light.

'I see what you mean,' said his mother. 'I didn't really notice them when you brought them here, I was so happy to see you.'

'Will you take them to the sultan and ask him for his daughter's hand in marriage?' pleaded Aladdin.

'Oh my son, how can I? He might kill us both for my impudence!'

'If you don't, I shall die,' said Aladdin.

So his mother put the jewels in a basket, covered them carefully with a white cloth, and set off to try to get an audience with the sultan. There were hundreds of people waiting in the reception hall, and the most important were seen first. She came home in the evening exhausted, having failed. For seven days she stood in the great hall

from morning until night, awaiting her turn. Finally the sultan said to his vizier, 'Bring that woman to me. She has been waiting far too long.' The vizier did as he was told.

'What is it you want?' the sultan asked Aladdin's mother kindly.

'Please forgive me, your majesty, but my son wishes to marry your daughter.'

The sultan tried to hide a laugh, and the vizier giggled. 'Show me what you have in your basket,' said the sultan, for he did not want to hurt the woman's feelings.

She lifted the cloth, and the jewels sparkled like stars. 'I've never seen a gem to equal any one of these, have you?' the sultan said to his vizier.

'No,' said the vizier. 'But I thought your daughter was promised to my son.'

'Not exactly promised,' said the sultan. 'We only discussed it once!'

The sultan thought for a while. He wasn't very fond of the vizier's son, and he found the idea of this woman's son, with his priceless jewels, fascinating. 'I'll tell you what,' he said to the vizier, 'If in three months time you can produce a better offering than this, my daughter shall belong to your son. In the meantime, my dear woman,' he said, turning to Aladdin's mother, 'you may assume she will marry your son.'

Aladdin's mother rushed home to tell him the good news, and they rejoiced together.

But the jealous vizier managed to persuade the sultan that Aladdin must be a scoundrel even to *have* such jewels to offer. 'Let my son marry your daughter before the three months are up,' he begged the sultan. 'My son has elegance and charm! You won't regret it.'

The sultan, who was a good man, but weak, allowed himself to be persuaded, and one day when Aladdin's mother was out shopping she overheard talk of a great wedding that was to take place the very next day.

'Whose wedding?' she asked.

'Don't you know? The princess is marrying the vizier's son!'

When she told Aladdin, he nearly died of grief. But there was no time for him to lie around starving himself if he was to win the hand of the princess. Aladdin waited until the wedding feast was over and the princess and her husband had retired to bed. Then he sent the genie of the lamp to the royal palace, instructing him to pick up the bed the newly-weds were lying in and bring it to his house.

The genie did as he was told. Then Aladdin asked the great creature to carry the husband far out in the country and leave him in a field. Aladdin then lay down in the dark next to the terrified princess, who could not even see him and could not guess what had happened to her.

'Don't be afraid,' Aladdin whispered. 'I will do you no harm. See, I have put my sword between us. You can go to sleep now.'

'What has happened to my husband?' asked the poor girl.

'Do you love your husband?' asked Aladdin.

'Well, no,' the princess said. 'But I wouldn't wish any harm to come to him.'

'No harm will come to him,' said Aladdin. 'Goodnight, princess.' And he turned around and went to sleep.

The vizier's son, meanwhile, was having a miserable night out in the cold, and he was very uncomfortable lying on the bumpy ground. But when morning came the genie picked him up and took him back to the palace, and the genie delivered the sleeping princess to her own room as well.

The same thing happened the next night, and the night after that. The vizier's son decided that he could stand it no longer, and he said he wanted the marriage annulled. The sultan was disgusted with the young man for not being satisfied with his lovely daughter, and willingly granted the annulment. So the princess was free again.

Aladdin was full of glee. After the three months were up, he sent his mother to the sultan again. 'My son is ready to marry your daughter now!' she said brightly, as though she knew nothing of the other marriage, which had begun and ended so quickly. The sultan was relieved – he had forgotten all about Aladdin, and had been afraid that nobody would ever want to marry his daughter since she had been rejected by the vizier's son.

But the vizier was not so pleased. He couldn't bear to give up all hope that his son and the princess would some day be reunited. He whispered to the sultan, 'I still don't trust Aladdin. Why don't you test him before you give him your only daughter? My son may be a little strange, but at least he has elegance and charm, and I'm sure he will grow to appreciate your daughter one of these days.'

The sultan glared at the vizier, but he was a bit weak. And he was worried about Aladdin – after all, he had not even met the young man, and his mother was not very impressive.

'Ask him to send you forty bowls of precious jewels carried by forty girls, and forty vases full of nectar carried by forty slaves,' whispered the vizier.

The sultan asked Aladdin's mother to pass the message on to her son.

'So now what are we going to do?' the woman cried in despair. 'Even if you were to go back to that wretched cave and get more jewels, where could you possibly find forty

slaves and forty girls? Oh, we are lost.'

'Don't worry, mother,' said Aladdin. 'There is no problem.' He rubbed the lamp, and once again the genie appeared. 'So many strange things keep happening,' Aladdin said to the genie. 'The vizier is making it all very complicated.'

'What is your wish?' boomed the genie.

'Well, if you could organize forty slaves and forty girls, to carry golden vases full of nectar and bowls full of precious jewels as lovely as the ones I found in the cave, I'd be grateful. Their clothing and hairstyles and so forth I leave entirely up to you.'

The genie disappeared, and in his place there the slaves and girls all were, crowding the house and spilling over into the street. Aladdin's mother led them straight to the sultan's palace. Imagine the sultan's amazement when he saw them appear so soon after he had requested them! And imagine the vizier's fury! 'Your son may marry my daughter this very night,' said the sultan to Aladdin's mother.

She rushed home, and as soon as he saw her face Aladdin knew that the sultan had given in at last. 'You are to be married this very night!' his mother cried. 'What am I to wear?' But by this time she probably realized the genie could solve that sort of problem.

Aladdin rubbed his lamp and the genie appeared. 'What is your wish?' he roared.

'I would like a scented bath, and my mother would too. Then we would like to be dressed in clothes befitting the occasion. Could we have a stallion as wonderful as the sultan's, but not more wonderful, for me to ride, and six beautiful slave girls to accompany mother, and some other slaves to carry ten thouand pieces of gold in ten purses for the sultan?'

No sooner said than done. When Aladdin was bathed and dressed he looked like the most magnificent of princes, and as he rode through the streets on his stallion, none of his friends recognized him, though he smiled and waved to them. His mother, walking along in her finery with her attendants surrounding her, was so happy she almost danced. And when they arrived at the palace, the princess, who was watching the procession from a window, gasped and blushed with joy to see her handsome husband-to-be. The sultan himself was quite

overwhelmed. Aladdin gave him the gold, and they embraced. The sultan marvelled at Aladdin's princely bearing, his cultured speech, his wit, and his mother's queenly dignity. The old lady had been transformed! Then a great feast was held. Musicians played, people danced and sang, and hundreds of dishes, each more succulent than the one before it, were served, along with the most marvellous wines. Everyone in the city was invited, and the festivities went on until late in the night. Aladdin and the princess sat in the midst of the crowd, gazing with wonder into each other's eyes.

'I love you,' said Aladdin.

'I love you, too,' said the princess. 'It is strange, but your voice sounds familiar to me. Have we met before? I don't remember *seeing* you!'

'You haven't seen me before,' said Aladdin.

'Let the ceremony now take place!' cried the sultan.

'It would be wonderful to marry the princess now,' said Aladdin, 'but first, oh sultan, I must ask if you would grant me a plot of land on which I can have a palace built which will be worthy of your daughter.'

'I have many plots of land which I could offer you,' said the sultan, 'but how would you like to build on the land right in front of my palace? Then we could always be dropping in on each other.'

'That would be perfect,' replied Aladdin. 'I am grateful to your majesty for wanting us nearby.'

So after the wedding, Aladdin summoned the genie and asked him to build a wonderful palace, fit for his new wife. 'How it should look I leave entirely up to you,' said Aladdin, 'for I know little about these things.'

The genie nodded and smiled, and in the twinkling of an eye there stood a palace as beautiful as the sultan's, but not as big. It was of marble, with precious stones set around the arches. The inside walls were covered in magnificent tapestries, and on the floors were the most exquisite carpets. Crystal windows, beautifully carved, filtered the light into the rooms. There were seven bedrooms, two living-rooms, a large kitchen filled with shining gold and silver pots and pans, and other rooms for sewing, playing games, listening to music, and eating. Every piece of furniture was a delight to the eye. It was quite a palace. Outside, a beautiful garden full of rare and sweet-smelling flowers and fruit trees appeared, and there were stables for about fifteen horses. Beyond the stables appeared a lake, on it a little boat was moored. The vizier, looking from a distance, turned green as grass with envy, but the sultan was delighted. The princess was pleased too, but she was less interested in the palace than in just being with Aladdin.

Remember the sorcerer from Morocco, who had taken Aladdin to the cave in the first place? Well, he was back in Africa having a terrible time. Things were going so badly for him that one day he decided it might cheer him up to see exactly what had happened to Aladdin, whether the flesh had yet rotted from his bones as he lay in the cave. So the magician sprinkled some incense into his samovar and said a spell. Imagine his surprise when a picture rose out of it, not of Aladdin lying dead, but of Aladdin living happily and in great splendour with a lady who was clearly a princess! The sorcerer raged and fumed and stamped on his spell-book and kicked his cat, but he couldn't change the picture, and he knew that his spells never lied, and that the picture was a true picture of Aladdin. He also realized that the only way Aladdin could possibly have married the most beautiful princess in the world was by using the magic lamp.

'So,' he mused, 'the boy was not so stupid. He rubbed the ring and got himself home; he rubbed the lamp and got himself everything he could possibly want. *My* ring! *My* lamp! It's unbearable, atrocious. Criminal. He must be the wickedest young man in the world. I hate him!' and he kicked the cat again.

Then the sorcerer set out for China. It wasn't so easy now that he didn't have his magic ring anymore. Instead of taking minutes, it took months for him to get there. When he arrived in the city where Aladdin lived, he felt exhausted and very old. He heard everywhere talk of the sweet, kind, beautiful princess and her gentle, loving, handsome husband. The sorcerer turned as green as an evergreen tree, he was so jealous. But then he heard some good news – that Aladdin was away for eight days on a fishing trip.

'I wonder if he took his lamp with him? Probably not, since if the boat tipped over the lamp would be lost. My luck is changing!' He rubbed his hands with glee, and jumped up and down.

'What are you so excited about?' asked a passing woman.

'I'm just so delighted to hear that the princess has married a good man!' he said. The woman smiled and walked on.

But after he stopped rejoicing, he started to worry. Although he was a magician, he wasn't a very powerful magician, now that he'd lost his ring. He couldn't, for instance, transport himself into the palace. 'How will I get that lamp?' he kept asking himself. 'I'm sure it's in the palace somewhere, but how do I get it?'

For days he walked up and down the city streets, racking his brain to figure out a way to get the lamp. Suddenly, at noon on the fifth day, he stopped short in front of a shop. It was a lamp shop! Quickly he went in and bought all the shiny new lamps he could see. Then he trudged off to the neighbourhood of the palace with his lamps in a big wheelbarrow.

'New lamps for old!' he cried, 'New lamps for old!' People clustered around him. 'He's crazy!' they said, but they were happy enough to exchange their rusty old lamps for his bright new ones. But nobody came out of Aladdin's palace. The magician began to worry again. What if he got rid of all his lamps without the princess noticing him? He raised his voice and shouted at the top of his voice, 'New lamps for old! New lamps for old!'

The princess was inside the palace covering her ears. 'What is that racket?' she asked her servant. 'Is there any way we can get it to stop?'

'Some fool is exchanging new lamps for old ones,' shouted her maid. 'Do you have any old lamps you want to get rid of?'

'If he'll stop making noise and get away from my gates, I'll gladly exchange an old lamp for a new one – I'd give him a new lamp for an old one if I could get rid of him that way! There's a lamp in one of the spare rooms he can have. Give it to him, and tell him to go away.'

So the servant took Aladdin's magic lamp and gave it to the magician in exchange for a shiny new one. 'Now go away,' she said, but the magician didn't need to be told. As soon as he got his hands on Aladdin's lamp, he dropped the handles of his wheelbarrow and ran away as fast as he could. He ran all the way to the desert that lay beyond the city, and, when he was sure he was alone, rubbed the lamp with trembling fingers. Instantly, the genie appeared.

'What is your wish?' he boomed in an angry voice. The poor genie could not choose his master.

'Take me, the princess and Aladdin's palace to Africa at once!' cried the magician. The genie had no choice. He lifted the magician up on his own head, grabbed the palace with the poor princess inside, and flew away over land and sea to Africa.

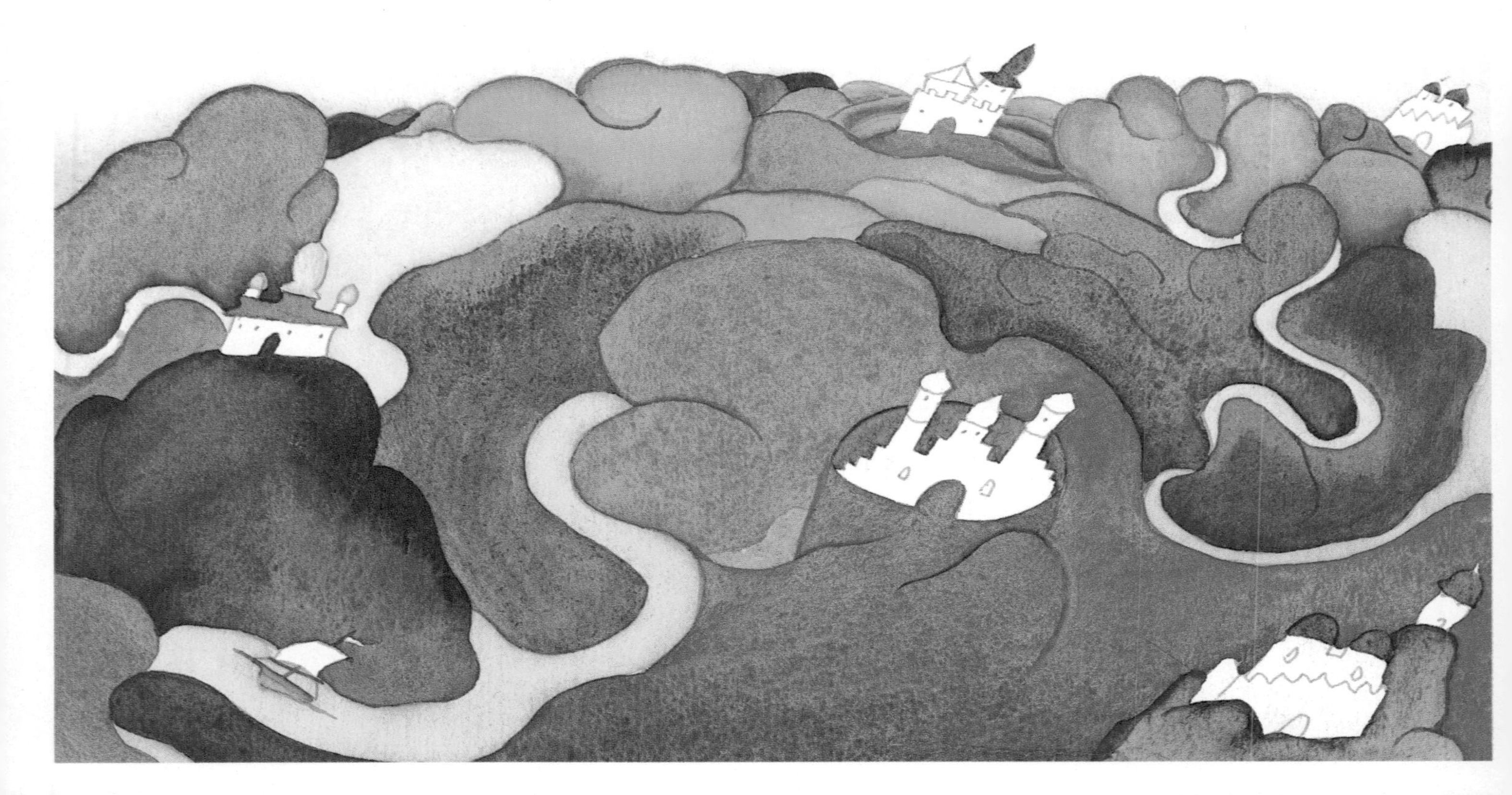

The princess, from the moment she was lifted into the sky, never stopped crying and calling her husband's name. But to no avail. She pined away in her palace in Morocco, and refused to be comforted.

When the sultan woke up the morning after the dreadful trick had been played, he jumped out of bed and went to the window to wave good morning to his daughter, as he always did. He was going to invite her for lunch, since her husband was away and he thought she might be feeling lonely. But when he looked out the window he saw nothing. He rubbed his eyes and looked again. Nothing. 'I must be dreaming!' he said, but he knew he wasn't.

He ran downstairs to get the vizier. 'Come upstairs with me immediately,' said the sultan, 'and tell me what you see!' He fleetingly wondered why he always went to the vizier for advice, when he didn't even trust the vizier.

The vizier followed him up to his bedroom. They went to the window. 'What do you see?' asked the sultan anxiously.

'I see a big garden, stables and a lake,' said the vizier, smugly.

'And what else?' asked the sultan.

'Nothing, really,' said the vizier. 'You see, your majesty, you've been duped by that scoundrel, Aladdin. I told you so.'

Meanwhile, Aladdin was on his way home. A few miles outside the city, he was stopped and seized by six men, and chained, and thrown on the back of a cart. 'What are you doing?' he shouted, but they only replied, 'We act on the sultan's command. You are to be executed.' They delivered him to the sultan, who cried, 'What have you done with my daughter?'

'What do you mean? Where is she?' Aladdin was beside himself with anxiety.

The sultan led him to his bedroom window. 'Where is my wife?' groaned Aladdin, 'where is my home?'

'Supposing you tell *me!*' snapped the sultan.

But Aladdin could not, and the vizier, delighted, arranged an execution. Aladdin was taken onto the balcony of the sultan's palace to await his death.

But when the people in the street below saw Aladdin in chains, and when they saw two executioners sharpening their swords, they raised a hue and cry and stormed the palace. 'Let Aladdin go!' they cried. 'Aladdin is a good and just man! If you kill him, there will be civil war! We will kill everyone in your palace!'

The sultan had no choice but to stop his executioners, and he unchained Aladdin. 'If you don't bring back my daughter, I hope you die a hundred times over,' he snarled, and the vizier nodded, and said, 'Yes, yes!'

'Give me forty days to find her and get her back,' said Aladdin. 'If I fail, you are more than welcome to kill me, for life without her means nothing to me.'

Then he went off into the desert by himself, and wept. He wrung his hands, and by chance he rubbed the magic ring, which he had forgotten all about, though it was always on his finger. The genie of the ring appeared.

'Where can I take you?' asked the genie, for, as you may remember, taking people places was that genie's particular speciality.

'Oh take me to my wife,' cried Aladdin. Suddenly, there he was in Africa, in his own palace, standing before his weeping wife.

'Aladdin, you found me!' she cried.

'Of course I did!' he said, embracing her, 'and now we have to find a way to get out of here. Where are we, anyway?'

'In Morocco, I think,' she said. 'I was brought here by a horrible and evil man.'

'I know the man,' said Aladdin, grimly. He thought for awhile, and finally said, 'I know how we'll get the lamp back. I'll hide, and you invite that man into your chamber. Be very sweet to him.'

'Oh, Aladdin, I *can't* be sweet to him!' cried his wife.

'It's all right, I'll be right here to protect you. It's the only way. Now listen carefully to me. You must ply him with wine, speaking kindly to him, until he falls asleep. Everything will be all right.'

The princess did as she was told. The sorcerer drank three jugs full of wine, and toppled to the floor, fast asleep.

'Oh, Aladdin!' said the princess, 'how I have missed you! I thought I would never see you again! He wanted me to marry him! I was so scared. How is my father? We must go, my love, before this dreadful man wakes up!'

'Yes,' said Aladdin. 'But first, I must take the magic lamp away from him. I am sure he has it on him somewhere.' Aladdin found the lamp wrapped in the magician's robe. 'How wonderful to see this lamp again!' he murmured.

'If you had only told me it was a magic lamp...' said his wife.

'Oh, my darling, you are so right. I will always tell you everything from now on. But I was afraid you wouldn't love me if you knew that I created the palace and everything by magic.'

'I would love you no matter what,' said the princess.

Aladdin rubbed the lamp and the genie appeared, looking very happy. 'What is your will?' he boomed.

'Please could you take us back to China as soon as possible?' said Aladdin.

It would be impossible to describe the feelings of the sultan when he saw the palace in its place again, a few moments later. And a few moments after that, his daughter was in his arms. The three of them laughed, and cried, and hugged one another, and swore never to be separated again. As for the vizier, he finally gave up and left, unnoticed.

Aladdin and the princess found a secret place in which to keep the lamp, and they never told another soul about it. The wicked magician stayed in Africa, and lived miserably forever after.

Sindbad the Sailor

Once upon a time, a few hundred years ago, there lived in the city of Baghdad a poor porter named Sindbad, who spend all his time carrying heavy loads from one end of the city to the other. One day, the heat overcame him and he sat down to recover in the shade of an enormous mansion. As he sat there, he was filled with a sense of peace for the first time in years. Delicate perfumes from the flowers in the garden combined with the smell of roast meat surrounded him. Beautiful soft music engulfed him, and he seemed to be in a dream. But suddenly he roused himself, straightened his aching back and rubbed his head with bony fingers. 'Why am I sitting here happily?' he cried, 'Why am I fooling myself? All that I smell, all that I hear, all that I see, I will never come close to!

Ah, it is unfair that some people are born to such luxury, and never have to do a thing with their lives except lie around and eat and drink and listen to music. Their only work is to amuse one another. They can fall asleep when it's hot. Why wasn't I given a life like that? Why should I have to work all day and fall into bed at night on a half empty belly? There is something wrong with a world that allows these differences.'

Suddenly an old man appeared before him. 'Won't you come and sit in my garden with me for a while?' he said. 'You must be tired if you've been carrying that heavy load.'

'Who are you?' asked the porter.

'I am Sindbad the sailor. And who, may I ask, are you?'

'Sindbad the porter,' said Sindbad.

'Fascinating! A strange coincidence!' said the other Sindbad. 'I couldn't help overhearing you just now –'

Sindbad the porter blushed and hung his head. 'I'm sorry I said those things. I didn't realize I would be heard. I forgot myself.'

'It's quite all right. But come in and let me tell you about myself. Then maybe you'll see that I earned my riches the hard way.'

And he proceeded to tell this story:

★ ★ ★ ★ ★

I came of a wealthy family, as you have guessed. But that is not why I am here today, living in all this luxury! For when I was a young man, my parents died, and although they left me quite a lot of money, I frittered most of it away. Finally, I decided to sell my household possessions and go to sea on a merchant ship. I had always loved the sea, and I was restless and needed to travel, to see new places and new faces. So I bought a lot of spices and joined a merchant ship which was bound for exotic lands.

For three months we sailed from island to island, stopping at each for a few days to trade our wares and enjoy ourselves. It was a pleasant life. Then one day we landed on an island that seemed different from the others. There were date palms growing on the beaches, but the ground was very smooth, and we saw no people and no animals. Still, we were tired, and so we decided to stop there and rest, even if it wasn't the most wonderful island in the world.

So we got our food and wine off the ship, and sat down to a nice picnic. The island was strangely quiet, and we started joking about how all the people and animals must have run away when they saw us land, because we were so ugly. Suddenly the island trembled. 'What is this, an earthquake?' shouted one of our men. Another man plunged headlong into the sea, and surfaced to yell, 'No, it's not an earthquake, it's a whalequake! The island isn't an island, it's a whale!' That whale must have been asleep for such a long time that trees took root and grew on its back. But we had woken it up with our noise. And when it was awake, it was really awake!

The next thing we knew, we were all in the water. The other men managed to get back to the boat (I found out later) but I was carried out to sea. Fortunately, I came upon a piece of wood which I clung to for dear life. I floated up and down on the waves all that day and far into the night.

I knew I couldn't hold on much longer to my piece of wood – my hands were getting numb from the cold. So I prepared to die. But just as I had given up all hope, I drifted towards a pot bouncing along on the top of the waves – a pot big enough for me to fit into! I managed to clamber into it, and soon collapsed. When I woke up in the morning, the sun was shining, the sky was blue, and it seemed as though the sea had stopped in its tracks. I wasn't moving at all.

'Maybe I'm dead,' I thought, 'and this is heaven.' I peered over the edge of my pot – and saw, not blue, but yellow. I had been washed up onto an island!

My body was so sore that for some hours I stayed curled up in the pot. Finally, though, I got so hungry I had to climb out. My feet were swollen from being so long in the freezing water, and I had to crawl on my hands and knees.

But I was lucky. There turned out to be plenty of fruit trees further inland, and a fresh-water spring, so I was able to eat and drink and bathe my poor aching limbs, and I recovered quickly. I still went back to my pot at night – I guess I had grown fond of it, I saw it as a kind of home.

One day, I woke up to see a most beautiful and noble-looking mare tied to a stick which had been hammered into the ground. When she saw me, she neighed a loud, terrified neigh, and immediately a man emerged from under the ground.

'What are you doing here?' he shouted. I told him all about what had happened to me in the last few days – or was it weeks? – and he was amazed at my luck.

'Now I've answered your question, it's your turn to answer mine,' I said. 'What is this beautiful mare doing here tied to a stick in the middle of the desert?'

'Ah,' said the man, 'that is easy to explain. In fact, if you stay for awhile, you will see for yourself. I am one of the grooms of the king of this island. His hobby is collecting exotic horses. Every month, on the night of the full moon,

the grooms tether the mares on the beach and then dig holes in the ground and hide. Pretty soon, all the sea-horses who have made their homes around this island come rolling up on shore. They are wonderful creatures, jade green, with sharp fins on their backs. They fall in love with the mares, and the mares fall in love with them, and they mate. The mares want to run away with them into the sea, but of course they can't, because they are tied to sticks.

Poor mares, we feel sorry for them – but after all, if they did follow the sea-horses into the sea, they would drown. The sea-horses don't feel sorry for the mares, though. They don't understand that the mares can't run away. So they start kicking them and butting them with their fins, trying to force them to come with them. When the sea-horses start to attack their mates, the other grooms and I jump out of our holes and beat them with sticks. Then they rush back into the sea, and disappear until the full moon comes round again. Then new mares are tied to sticks, and so it goes, on and on. The mares bear the most beautiful little colts in due course, and the king is very happy.'

I stayed and watched while all this took place, and I must admit I felt very sorry for the mares and the sea-horses.

'I should like to meet your king,' I said, and the groom said he would be happy to take me to him. The king greeted me kindly and asked me to tell him how I came to be there. I told him my story – I was getting quite good at telling it – and we ate and drank together. We became friends, and the king begged me to stay on the island.

There were so many strange animals on and around that island! There was a fish with the head of a bird who sometimes swam up to the shore. He was a very friendly creature, and he liked to be fed worms. Then there were rhinoceroses, huge black creatures who looked as though they would love to eat people; in fact they ate only grass. They had one horn sticking up from their noses. The king even had a rhinoceros for a pet. He was a ferocious-looking beast, but he wouldn't hurt a flea. He did tricks on special occasions, and all the people on the island would gather round to watch him dance, or balance a bowl of oranges on his horn. Sometimes when he was doing tricks I noticed that he had sad eyes, and I felt very sorry for him. I was glad that I was a man and not a rhinoceros.

I stayed for a long time on that island, and it was a happy time for me. The king appointed me controller of shipping, and I came to be his closest friend. The people grew fond of me because I wasn't proud. There were plenty of women who would have been more than happy to marry me, and I was never short of money. My life was almost too good to be true. I had friends, I had work that I enjoyed, I was rich. But after a few years I grew restless. I felt a great yearning to be at sea again. I mentioned this to a jester with whom I spent a lot of evenings.

'Isn't it funny!' said the jester. 'If you have nothing, you want everything. If you have everything, you want to lose it. Everybody wants what he doesn't have.'

'Do you think the king will be angry if I tell him I want to leave?' I asked.

'No,' said the jester. 'The king is never angry.'

So I told the king how happy I had been on his island, but that I felt I must depart.

'Please,' he said, 'Don't apologize! I always knew you would go sooner or later. You are not the kind of man who stays forever in one place. It is strange, when I was your age I always wanted to travel, the way you do. Now, every time I leave the island I wish I could be back on it again!'

He gave me a whole heap of gold in a red silk sack decorated with black trees, and he gave me his best camel as well. I was touched by his generosity.

The camel and I boarded a ship and eventually landed on another island. It looked like an interesting place, full of wild plants growing up the sides of steep mountains, and I decided to stay for a while. My camel carried me about for a week and we saw nothing but plants, trees, mountains and sky. Then one day we found ourselves approaching something that looked like the sun, only it was too white and not bright enough. Perhaps it was the dome of a great building? We went closer.

I left my camel to have a rest and a drink of water, and walked boldly up to the white dome. Suddenly it burst open! It was not a dome at all, but a huge egg, so huge that all the rest of the eggs in the world put together would not have equalled it in size. Out popped a baby bird. Baby! It was a baby as big as a hill. Then I remembered the tales sailors had told me of the marvellous giant bird called a roc. In the distance I saw the mother roc approaching, flying through the air to bring her baby its meal. And what

do you think the meal was? A worm, or a grub? A crumb of bread? No, it was an elephant. She put the elephant in her baby's outstretched beak, and he ate it as though it were merely the first course of a meal. Yet I realized as I watched this giant of a baby that however big he was he still looked like a baby.

Then I remembered something the king of the last island had told me. The rhinoceros, when it is feeling playful, sometimes picks an elephant up on its horn and dashes about with it, just to scare it. But the elephant is too heavy for the rhinoceros after a while, so they fall to the ground together. Then along comes the giant roc, who picks them both up and carries them off to her baby....

It certainly made me feel scared, knowing that the roc chick was probably still hungry after eating only one little elephant. I was the next creature the mother roc would see, and though I would be only a morsel, I was sure I would be a tasty one, worth picking up.

So I kept as still as a stone. How was I to get away from this awful island? Why, oh why had I ever left the peaceful island where the king was my friend and the rhinoceroses danced? Why had I ever started travelling in the first place? Why hadn't I settled down in my father's lovely house in Baghdad? I suffered and blamed myself and suffered some more.

But when the roc and her baby finally fell asleep in each other's wide wings, I stopped worrying and started thinking. And then I had a splendid idea. The best way to keep myself from being discovered by the mother roc was to hide myself *on her.* How could I do this? Easy.

I grabbed hold of her tail feathers and wrapped some of them around me. In fact I did my best to look like a tail feather myself. Anyway, her tail was such a great distance from her head that it didn't seem likely that she would see me buried there in her feathers, unless she was actually looking for me. I didn't think she would smell me. Anyway, can birds smell? I curled up like a feather and wondered about that until I fell asleep, and I didn't wake up till dawn.

I was awakened by a whoosh of air. We were climbing the sky. It was lucky I had wrapped myself up well in the feathers! I held on for dear life after the feathers unwound around me, and we sailed high up in the sky. I gave a thought to my poor camel. I hoped he would manage to escape somehow from that island. Or maybe the roc would find him too bumpy to eat.

The roc flew so high that when I looked down the seas looked like puddles and the mountains like anthills. I was scared. Then suddenly we swerved, and I saw, below, a herd of elephants. From that distance they looked like little ivory elephants from a charm bracelet. The roc flew straight at them, and they got bigger and bigger. I knew she was planning to pick one up for her baby. As soon as her feet touched the ground, I let go of her tail and ran, as fast as my legs would carry me.

After my escape from the roc mother, I was found by a bunch of wicked pirates and taken to Siam to be sold as a slave. Fortunately, a rich merchant bought me, and he saw that I was intelligent and decided to give me a chance to prove myself.

'Are you good with a bow and arrow?' he asked, and I replied that I was.

'Then go to the forest every day, and climb a tree, and wait for the elephant herd to go by, and shoot me down one elephant each day, so that I can have his ivory tusks to sell.'

I didn't like the idea of killing elephants, but I had no choice, so every day for two weeks I sat in a tree and waited for the herd to trample by. I would shoot one down with several well-placed arrows, and wait for the rest to run

away. Then I would go back to fetch my master, and together we would remove the tusks from the poor dead elephant. My master was pleased with me.

Just as I was beginning to think the elephants were very stupid to fall for such a ploy, something happened that made me think they were more intelligent that most of the *people* I have met. One day, the whole herd surrounded my tree and started trumpeting so loudly I thought I would go deaf. When one of them wound his trunk around the tree and uprooted it, I thought I was to die, and I felt I deserved to die as well, for hadn't I killed many of them? But a second elephant gently picked me from the branch, and holding me carefully in his trunk he carried me away, with all the other elephants following after him.

After hours which seemed like days, the elephant put me down, as kindly as a mother puts a child down to rest, and they all turned around and disappeared into the jungle.

I looked around in amazement. As far as I could see in every direction were strewn the huge white bones and tusks of elephants. This was their burying ground! I realized that the elephants were trying to show me a way to get their tusks without killing them. I made my way back to my master's house, and told him of my discovery. He returned to the burial ground with me and could hardly believe his eyes. 'You have made my fortune,' he said, but I told him that it was the elephants themselves who had made his fortune.

Together we collected the tusks for weeks on end. My master freed me, rewarding me with a large fortune of my own, for he was a good and generous man.

I continued to travel, and soon landed on an island full of the most elegant people. The king befriended me, and offered me a beautiful and wealthy bride. I thought it might be time for me to settle down and raise a family, so I accepted, and I lived happily with her for some months.

But one day, the wife of one of our neighbours got ill and died. I went to comfort the husband, and found him beside himself with grief, wailing and screaming and tearing out his hair.

'Come, man,' I said, 'I understand how much you must be suffering, but you must pull yourself together now. You will find another wife! You have to go on living!'

'Go on living!' he replied. 'That's just the problem! Don't you know that it is the custom in this country when a woman dies to bury her husband with her?'

I went pale with horror, and started to take the greatest possible care of my own dear wife. But alas, she was stricken down by the same illness, and within a few days she was dead.

How could I escape this terrible island before being buried alive? There seemed to be no way. The neighbours came to my house – indeed, I was a man of such importance that the king himself came with all his ministers – and with lots of tears and apologies they lowered me into the freshly dug pit where my wife and all the other wives and their husbands were buried. The darkness closed around me as though I were in a tomb. I *was* in a tomb! I trembled from head to foot.

Just as I began to give up all hope, an owl flew into the hole, which had not yet been closed up. He looked perfectly contented, as though he knew exactly where to go — as though there *were* somewhere to go. I picked myself up off the ground and followed him. He flew along slowly — he seemed to know he was my guide. He went through a crack in the wall of the cavern, and I squeezed in after him. We went, it seemed, miles, and just as I was beginning to feel I couldn't breathe any more, I saw a light ahead. We came out onto the seashore and the owl flew away. He had saved my life.

As I stood in the sunshine on the shore, wondering what to do next, a gang of pirates leapt out at me from behind some rocks. More pirates! I began to feel that the world was full of pirates. They took me to their ship, and off we sailed, but they must have decided that I was a useless man, for they abandoned me at the next island. I was very grateful to them, and when I saw a huge castle rising up before my eyes, which seemed to be as big as the whole island, I was delighted.

The ivory gates to the castle were open, so I went in. I wandered around from one enormous room to another, hoping to find the people who lived there. I was wretchedly hungry and thirsty — I could not remember when I had last eaten. Everything in the castle was twenty

times larger than life. At first the place seemed like an abandoned city, for the tables were like houses without walls, and the chairs were lean towers. I came upon what at first seemed to be a short path leading nowhere – and then I realized it was the belt of a giant slung on the floor.

I began to get scared again. I had always loved adventure, but I was beginning to feel I had had enough for the time being. I thought of my poor wife, now dead. I remembered Baghdad, and my house there which I had left so long ago. 'I must be getting old,' I thought, 'for I want to go home.' Just then the room I was in trembled, and the torches on the walls flickered. In walked a giant so tall that I stood no higher than his ankle. I backed against a wall and gazed up at his face. He had only one gigantic eye. He sat down and poured himself some wine, and then more, and more, until he drank himself to sleep.

I quickly climbed up the table-leg and hid in the sugar-bowl. I was able to eat the sugar, which I sorely needed, and then, too exhausted to worry any more, I fell asleep.

I must have slept for a long time, because I woke up feeling as though I had just been born. I carefully lifted the lid of the sugar-bowl and peered out. There was no way, in that dark and dreary castle, of knowing whether it was day or night.

Then I heard a crash and the table shook. I knew I had been seen, and that the giant had pounded his fist on the table. I got out of the bowl, leapt to the floor – it was like jumping from a high window – and then started to run. It was strange, by this time I actually felt that I was a tiny little creature, and that everything around me was normal. I thought, 'This must be the way it is for a baby kitten when it sees people and furniture!' But the difference was, I could move very fast, unlike a baby kitten, and I also had a wonderful human mind. I was sure that I would be able to outwit the giant, as long as I could stay out from under his feet. He was tramping through the castle looking for me and roaring. At least he was easy to see and hear!

There was a pile of empty bottles in the corner of one room. I slithered into one and held my breath. He went right through that room like a storm.

So I was safe – but how long could I survive in the bottle? I decided not to think about it, and fell asleep once more. 'Anyway, I'm getting plenty of rest here!' I thought when I woke up. But just then I realized *why* I had woken up. I was moving, fast. The bottle was pitch black. Then I knew I was in the giant's hand. 'My time is up,' I thought. But I was in luck. He was just throwing bottles into the sea to amuse himself, it seemed, he didn't even notice me. So the next thing I knew, everything around me was blue.

I landed on a golden island, full of flowers, soft grass, and beautiful trees laden with fruits. The air was full of the songs of birds, and butterflies were wafting about in the gentle breeze. I was so happy! As I wandered about, feeling as though I were in a dream, I came upon a wretched old man at the bank of a river.

'Please,' he whined, 'help me across, for I cannot help myself.'

I took pity on him and hoisted him to my shoulders. Then he hooked his legs around my neck and nearly choked me. He would not let go his grip for an instant. When I begged him to stop, and told him he was killing me, he only laughed.

But I didn't die. I got used to my burden, though it was wearing me out. Day by day I walked up and down, looking for food, which was easy to find, and wondering how to get rid of the old man. One day, I grabbed some grapes from a vine, pressed them into a gourd, and left the gourd hanging from a tree. When I went back to collect it, a few days later, the juice of the grapes had turned to sweetest wine. I drank it, and almost forgot the hateful old man on my shoulders. I made more wine that very day, in the same way, but when I went back for it he seized the gourd and drained it. Then he fell from my shoulders, fast asleep. This time I had really been lucky! I ran away and met some men who told me that it was the Old Man of the

Sea who had clung to me. 'You are the first person ever to get away from him,' they marvelled.

Then they took me to a coconut grove and told me I could have all the coconuts I wanted. But how was I to get at them? Every tree was swarming with vicious-looking monkeys. Then I had an idea. I picked up a sea-shell and hurled it at a monkey. He grabbed a coconut and threw it at me. The battle continued this way for hours, and soon the ground was covered with coconuts. I ate my fill, and drank the delicious coconut milk. 'Thank you, monkeys!' I shouted happily.

After that I found again the men who had befriended me and they took me to the town on the centre of the island. It seemed that the people of that town had been longing for the coconuts, but no one had figured out a way to get them away from the monkeys. So I showed them what to do – but they were afraid of the monkeys! So every few days I went back alone to the coconut grove, threw shells at the monkeys (but not hard enough to hurt them) and waited for them to try to pummel me with coconuts. In fact I was usually able to dodge their blows, and was never worse than bruised.

I became rich once again, selling coconuts to the people of the town. It was a pleasant period. I set up a stall on the main street and worked there every afternoon. I got to know everyone that way. I bought myself a lovely white house near the port, and decorated it with beautiful carpets and exquisite furniture.

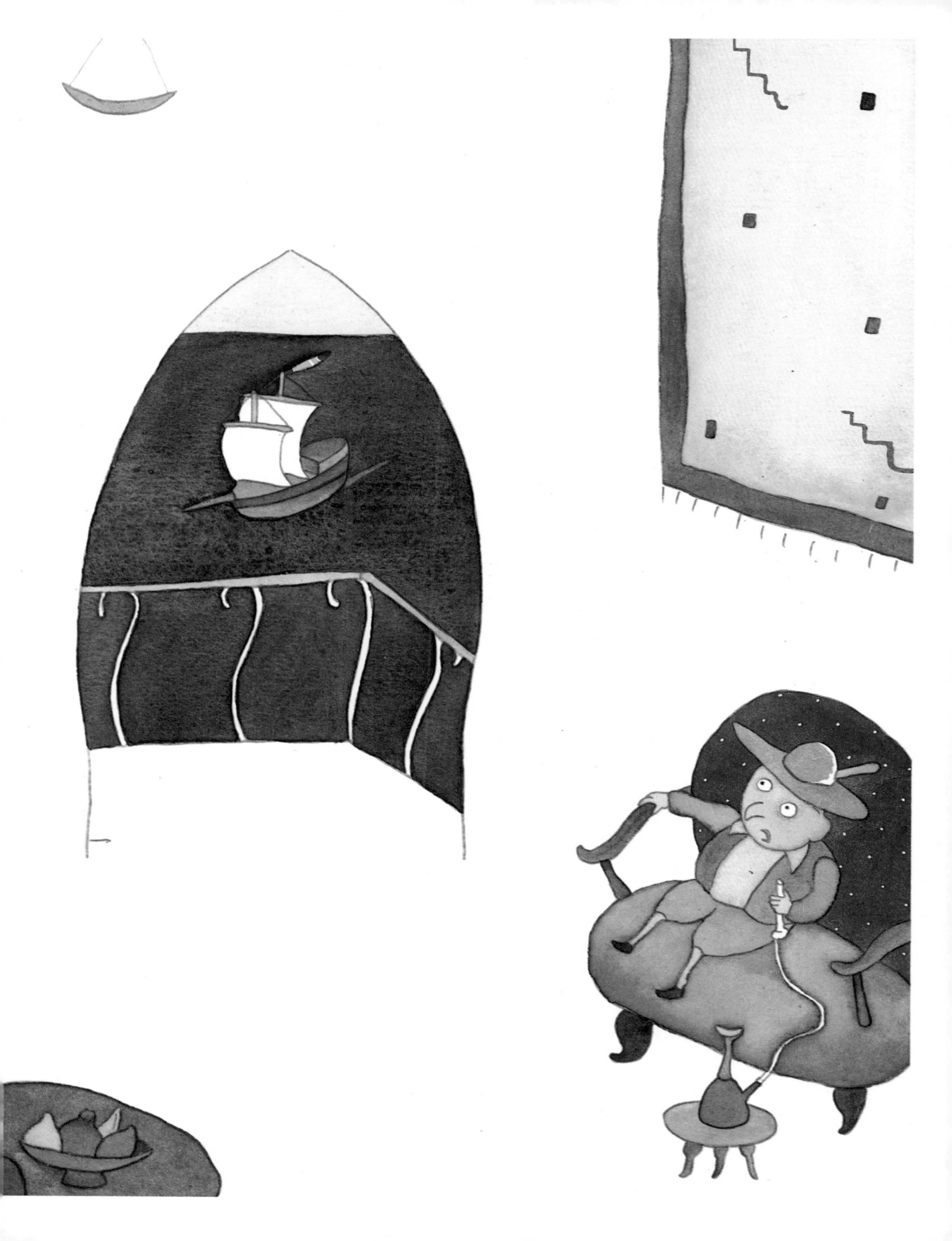

'I really am getting old!' I thought. 'Now if this house were in Baghdad I should be perfectly happy!' I considered marrying and settling down for good. But the women were so noisy, and they were too eager to have me. I began to feel restless again.

One day, I was sitting looking out to sea when I saw a ship which I knew was from Baghdad. I could tell by the flag. I was so excited! I packed my gold and a few precious objects and rushed to the harbour to greet my countrymen.

I told the captain and sailors that I too was from Baghdad. Somehow they looked familiar to me. We all embraced and had a meal together. As we ate and talked, I suddenly realized that they were the very men I had set out with on the ship, so many years ago. But they didn't recognize me. I had probably changed a lot. All those narrow escapes from death had probably aged me by about a hundred years.

The captain told me that they had been at sea for many, many years, and in all that time had suffered only one disaster, right at the beginning of their voyage. 'A man was lost. I still have his belongings,' he said sadly. 'He was a good man. I am hoping that some day we will find one of his relatives to give his things to. Come to think of it, you look a little bit like that man. You aren't an uncle of his or something, are you? His name was Sindbad.'

'I am that very Sindbad,' I replied. I described the belongings which I had left behind on the ship.

'Yes, that's exactly right!' cried the captain. He wept with delight, and I wept too, and then we all boarded the ship and returned to Baghdad together. It was an easy journey, and a happy one. After I got home, I vowed never to travel again, and I never have.

★ ★ ★ ★ ★

Sindbad the sailor was quiet for a while, as if he were still reliving his past. He looked at Sindbad the porter and smiled. 'So you see,' he said, 'I was not really born to the wealth I have now, I worked hard for it. But also, it is true that I was very lucky. And I wish you luck too.'

He filled Sindbad the porter's plate again, and poured him some more wine, and they sat together in a comfortable silence.